Destiny
Path of Life™

The Journey Begins

Joseph James

Destiny
Path of Life™
The Journey Begins

© 2009 Joseph James

ISBN: 978-0-9842422-0-7

Destiny Path Of Life™
Joseph James and Janiece (Jaan) Hartmann,
10455 N. Central Expy. #109-101,
Dallas, TX 75231, USA.

Visit us at: www.DestinyPathOfLife.com

CONTENTS

ACKNOWLEDGMENTS

To my wife, Janiece (Jaan), my precious princess, thank you for who you are and for your love and grace. I love you. May you continue to blossom, more and more, all the days of your life.

To my children, Desiree, Krystal, Lauren, Daniel, and my grandson Hunter, you are precious in my sight, I love you. May the Lord continually give you His best.

Thank you Krystal for creating all of the illustrations in this book. They are truly a wonderful gift. Continue to paint that which you see in the Spirit.

To my mom, Lily, you always believed in me, even when you didn't understand, thank you for everything. I love you. I believe the best is still ahead for you.

To Larry Larsen, my true father, you stood with this shattered reed through everything and no matter what came next, you were always there. Thank you, I love you.

I would like to thank Virginia Turner, Janiece's mom, for editing the earlier draft of this book and also Bob Turner, her dad for sharing your print expertise along with suggesting I include my poem, "I Wish." I love you both. Gin, I know you are in heaven now and finally free from pain.

I would like to thank George and Diane Senecal of Shining Light Ministries in Montrose, Colorado for accommodating me at their home. This gave me the time and space I needed to climb the mountain of the Lord, to get in His presence and commune with Him to write the first draft of this book among many other things. This is only the beginning of the journey.

I would like to thank Terry and Deborah Lewis for helping me get to Colorado to write the first draft and for the years of friendship.

I would like to thank everyone at City Church in San Antonio, Texas and Dennis Davis. I would also like to thank everyone else who has been instrumental in my life, including Mark Hiller, Cindy Gasch, Jess & Lucille Sapp, Dan & Lynda Kaspar, Cleo Wendell, and Connie Tillery. When our lives touch, we carry a little bit of each other with us wherever we go.

Thank you, Jackie Haag, of Mother's House Publishing. Without your help and encouragement, the journey would have been much more difficult. You are a special addition to our family. May this only be the beginning.

Most of all, I would like to thank the true author of this book, the Holy Spirit of God. I am just a servant of the Lord Jesus Christ. He alone deserves the credit and the glory. I put down on paper that which I believe I received from Him. May His Name be lifted up that He might draw all men unto Him and give them eternal life.

Thank you, Lord, for the beautiful Rocky Mountains and Your magnificent creation that never ceases to praise Your Majestic Name.

Thank you all from the fullness of my heart.

Joseph James

INTRODUCTION

Even though this book is written in an allegory fashion and is fiction, much can be acquired from its overall content. Each one of us travels a path in life to our own destiny. It is a choice we must make and there is a reality at the end. It is my desire that the reader asks himself/herself these questions. Where am I going? Where is my destiny? What is my definition of success? How will I get there? Will I take the time to search for the truth? What will it cost me? And in the end, was it worth it?

There is also an art print I have designed, "Destiny Path Of Life™," that can help one focus more clearly on their destiny. It will be available in the future from the address at the front of this book or go to the web site. It will also be helpful in the sequels to this book. Stay in touch to find out what is next on the Destiny Path Of Life™ web site. We have a blog on the site where we post messages of encouragement and understanding. Feel free to subscribe to it by RSS feed, by email, or just stop by the website at your convenience to read them. Use our form on the contact page to send us your stories, experiences and/or prayer requests.

May your journey in life be filled with peace, love, joy and hope. May you experience the narrow path of life and the friendship of the Lord Jesus Christ. May this book give you insight into your destiny and help you make the choices you need to make. I love this journey. I can truly say that it is the best thing that has ever happened to me and I hope to meet you on this path someday.

Joseph James

I WISH

I wish I could have grown up in the perfect
    family,
With a mother and father who love me so
    dearly,
With brothers and sisters who play instead
    of fight,
With each day a joyous adventure and peace
    through the night.

I wish I could have grown up in a world full
    of love,
One without wars, sin, grief, murder or
    strife,
Where it's safe to walk the streets and live in
    homes without locks,
Where everyone is full of love and each one
    like a friend.

This would be perfect, and then it would
    never end,
But in my world, a dream is all it will ever
    be,
Each one does his best just trying to make it
    through,

Yet, this one has the potential to be the greater of the two.

It's in these places, we find if true love exists,
Without mercy and forgiveness, it's only shallow at best.
How can we know its depths if it's never tested and tried?
It only shines and glows when, by the storm, it's purified.

I thought there were many who loved me or so they did say,
But when the storms came, they ran off and went away.
"Where are you? I thought you were my friend."
But they were all gone when I had looked again.

"Where did you come from, I didn't know you were there?
I thought I knew everyone, but what is your name?"
"I am the Lord, and I've always been near,

I have never left you, you are precious and
      dear."

My tears fell like rain as I ran to embrace,
His love surrounded me, His peace and
      grace.
He is all I need, we are together each day,
He healed all my wounds, in His presence
      I'll stay.

Now, I have new friends and I know them by
      name,
I know their limits and failures and I love
      them the same.
Humans are fragile and weak at their best,
But Jesus is perfect and His love passes the
      test.

Joseph James

The Journey Begins

Bill meets Mr. Wisdom
Illustration by - Krystal Morgan Stahl

Chapter 1

Bill and Mr. Wisdom Meet

Bill awakened with the sound of a lawn mower roaring to life in one of his neighbor's yards. He shook off the sleep as he raised his head up to look at his alarm clock. It was 7:30 and he was still in bed. He couldn't believe it. He was going to be late to the office. He had taken the whole weekend to go over his business plan and put together a strategy to get his company headed in a new direction and now he was going to get a late start. He quickly took a shower and grabbed a slice of toast as he put his jacket on and headed out the door. As he walked out of the gate of his front yard, he realized that he had forgotten to power off his entertainment system, so he hurried back inside to turn it off. He took a few minutes to check over everything before leaving again. As he closed the gate behind himself, he turned to walk down the sidewalk to his office just a few blocks down the street. He hoped that this was the last thing that would delay his long awaited plans. He was so eager to meet with his staff to show them the new direction he wanted to pursue.

As Bill was walking down the sidewalk, he greeted each of his neighbors by name. There was Sally tending to her flowers and Tom was across the street painting his front porch.

Bill continued on the next street and as he was approaching one of his favorite houses, he noticed that Mr. Wisdom was out on his front porch. He had not seen him in quite a while and was very excited to see him this morning. "Hello, Mr. Wisdom, how are you doing this morning? I haven't seen you in quite a while. It is so good to see you this morning." Bill exclaimed as he was walking so fast that he was almost running down the sidewalk.

Mr. Wisdom replied as he looked

up from the newspaper he was reading while he was swinging on his porch swing, "Hello Bill, I am doing just fine. It is really good to see you too. We just got back yesterday from a trip overseas. It is a beautiful sunny day today, isn't it? We have a new flock of ducks on the lake this morning and the birds have been singing their cheerful songs. It is so good to be back home. Where are you off to so fast this morning? It looks like you are going to a fire or something. Anything I need to know about?" He joked.

Stopping in his tracks and turning around, Bill decided he would take a little time out for a short chat. He was really eager to get to the office, but he had been meaning to stop and talk to Mr. Wisdom if the chance ever arose. He seemed to be a very intriguing man and Bill was really wanting to know more about him. Everyone in town loved and respected him and now the door was opening for him to get to talk to him. "Oh, I have all these appointments and schedules to make and it seems like there is never enough time to just relax. I just came up with a new business plan this weekend and I am eager to put it to the test. Busy, busy, busy! I don't know where the time goes. It seems like the days just keep getting shorter and shorter. I really didn't take the time to notice that the sun was shining today or for that matter, even to notice the beautiful songs of the birds. Tell me, Mr. Wisdom, how have you managed to achieve such success, and at the same time maintain so much peace and be so at ease about everything? I have watched you from a distance and you always seem to be at peace. It is like nothing ever stresses you out."

Mr. Wisdom had been hoping and praying for this moment to talk to Bill, so he put down his newspaper and walked over to the front gate of his yard. He was such a fine young man, but he was always on the run. He hoped that he would be able to spend some time with him to find out a little more about him. "Well son, I learned a long time ago that there were certain principles to follow and also that there was someone who knew more than

I did. I used to be as busy as you until one day like this, when someone came along and the words he spoke to me caused me to stop and think for a moment. It radically changed my life."

"Can you tell me about it," asked Bill? He tried to hide the eagerness inside, but was sure that Mr. Wisdom saw through it all. He had learned a lot of knowledge in school, but Mr. Wisdom's life seemed to contradict a lot of the things he had been taught. He would gladly give up the time it would take to get a glimpse of this mysterious man.

Mr. Wisdom looked curiously at Bill and said, "Well Bill, it may take a while and since you have such a busy schedule and all, maybe this isn't the most opportune moment. Why don't you take a moment and figure out when we might be able to get together? I'd hate to interrupt your schedule and all."

Bill thought for a moment, considered all the plans he had so carefully laid out, and then replied, "Yes, maybe you are right, but this moment is here now, and

I have been waiting for it for a long time and if I don't take it now, another one may never come along. My schedule and plans can wait for today because I really want to hear what it is that changed your life. I have seen other successful people too, but somehow you are different. You don't do things the way other successful people do. If you don't mind taking the time for me, I would sure like to hear your story. I can call my office and let Sherry know that I won't be in until later. They have enough to do to keep themselves busy anyway."

"Okay Bill," said Mr. Wisdom, "come with me out back so we can take in a view of the beautiful snow-capped mountains, the lake, and enjoy the fresh air while we talk. I so enjoy God's creation. I have even added a stone water fall next to the deck before we left so we can listen to the sound of trickling water while we talk. There is nothing like the sound of moving water. It seems to bring a peace to my soul."

Behind Mr. Wisdom's huge two-story, stone house was a mountain range of over 14,000 feet in elevation. The tops of the mountains had a glistening effect to them as the sun shone across their snow-covered peaks. Beyond the trees in the valley below, was a huge lake with hundreds of ducks swimming around. There were even some deer drinking at the water's edge. Spring was now in full bloom and the birds were fluttering about singing their wonderful songs. Here and there were flowers beginning to show their beauty and they were releasing fragrant perfumes into the air.

At the magnificent sight, Bill exclaimed, "This is a wonderful view! It is very majestic! You know something, Mr. Wisdom, I have been all around these mountains and the lake, but I have never really stopped to notice the beauty, nor have I seen it like I do today. It is like living in another world. Everything in my world is so stressful, noisy and busy. We are always trying to outdo someone else and the deadlines seem to arrive quicker with each project we begin. Thank you for setting aside some of your valuable time for me today. I really appreciate this. It is like a breath of fresh air. I really, really need this. I didn't know how much until just now." Bill was thinking that he could get used to just relaxing in this atmosphere. There was so much peace and quiet. He noticed that the noise that had been inside of his head was gone too. Everything was quiet. He could actually relax for a moment. This could become contagious.

Mr. Wisdom replied, "Well, you are welcome, son. There was a time about twenty years ago, when I didn't notice much of the beautiful things around me either. I was leaving my home town and heading for the big city to make a name for myself. I was not going to listen to anyone who told me no or to wait. I had made up my mind and no one was going to change it. Now, keep in mind that we didn't have all the gadgets we have now to keep me busy, but my mind was kept busy all the time, thinking only about success. I had this dream from an early age and I had made up my mind that when I was old enough I would pursue it with everything within me. I wanted to soar and live. I did not want to end up just working in a factory, doing the same old thing day after day for the rest of my life. I wanted something more. I wanted an adventure.

Bill turned around and sat down as he reached for the cup of coffee Mr. Wisdom had poured for him. Bill looked right into Mr. Wisdom's eyes as he asked, "What changed your life, because that is where I am now and if there is a better way, I would sure like to see it. I really don't like pain and discouragement and if there is any way to avoid it, I am all ears." Wow, this is the story I have been waiting for and here it is without my even having to ask for it, Bill thought to himself.

Mr. Wisdom took a sip of his coffee and then hesitated for a moment. He wanted to make sure that the words he chose would be the right ones and then went on, "Well, it was similar to the way we met, I suppose, at least for the fact that I was in a hurry too. I was driving through this town one day, heading for the big city, when I decided to stop at this café and get some breakfast and coffee for the journey ahead. I had been up most of the night driving so I needed some fuel in my car as well as in my stomach. I also needed something to help me stay awake. I went in and sat down at a small table over by the window and I noticed this older, distinguished-looking man looking at me. He really seemed genuinely interested in me eventhough I could not figure out why. By his appearance, it looked like he had a lot of money. As I looked around the café, I noticed that this was not a normal café. There was a lot of peace inside and everyone seemed at rest. Even the employees were speaking softly to each other. I marveled at what I saw and I was curious about what might be going on. It was later on that I learned that this was his café and he always mingled among his guests. Most of them knew each other on a first name basis so it was easy to distinguish the locals from those like me, who were just passing through."

"The town was down in a valley, so I was able to see it as I approached from a distance. It didn't look like there was really much to it, so I was grateful to find the café about midway through. It looked like one of those small country communities where everyone knows each other's business. There were only several gas stations, a firehouse, a small sheriff's office and a few other stores. There was a restaurant across the road, but there was something about this place that caught my attention. I decided I would check this place out first and if it didn't work out, I could always get back in my car and go across the street."

"The waitress was really pretty and she had a beautiful soft voice. They had a large variety of items on the menu, so it took a while for me to decide. I was actually somewhat embarrassed because it took so long for me to decide. She actually came over to my table twice before I made up my mind. I can remember to this day what I ordered though. They had a chicken fried steak that was the best I had ever eaten. It was so tender and full of flavor. It was like they saved the best for me. I also had two eggs, some hash browns and a few slices of a tomato."

"Right before I had finished eating, the

older gentleman got up from his chair, came over to my table and introduced himself to me. His name was Mr. Crossroads. He asked if he could join me, and I immediately said yes. I was really curious as to why he seemed so interested in me. I was also curious about this town and the people here. Who were they? It was so different from what I was accustomed to being around."

The Café along the way
Illustration by - Krystal Morgan Stahl

Chapter 2

Mr. Wisdom's Encounter With Mr. Crossroads

The stranger held out his hand and asked, "What is your name lad?"

"Mark Wisdom," replied Mark.

"My name is Thomas Crossroads. I saw you walk in like you were on your way to something so important that time was of the essence, so I thought I'd come over and see what's up."

With a slight smile of embarrassment, Mark replied, "Oh, I am just kind of in a hurry to get to the big city. I have wanted to go since I was a teenager and finally I have the opportunity. I have had these dreams for many years now. I have some ideas on how I might become successful and I'm eager to try them out. I want to make a difference in my life and in this world. At the end of my life, I want to be able to look back and say that it was worth it – I made it. I was successful."

Mr. Crossroads continued, with a grin on his face, "My! My! Looks like you have things pretty much in order, but tell me something, which road are you going to take?"

Mark, a little surprised at the unexpected question, replied rather quickly, "I don't know. You mean there is more than one. I guess I will take whichever one gets me there the fastest."

Mr. Crossroads took a long time to reply. It was as if he was carefully thinking about each word he wanted to say. "Whichever one gets you there the fastest. Um, um, I see! So you are not that interested in knowing what it might cost you and what you might find when you get there, huh?"

With a puzzled look on his face, Mark replied, "Well, I don't know, I haven't really thought about it that much. I didn't *even know there was more than one road until now. All I know is that I see the vision of my destiny and that is what I want. I want to be a success in this life. I want to make a difference." Mark was wondering what Mr. Crossroads was really talking about? Was there really more than one road out there or was he just leading him on? Could he trust him? After all, he had just met him and he was a stranger.*

"Well lad, if that is what you want, then I will leave you alone, but if you can spare a couple of days in your busy life, I have a friend that I would like you to meet. His house is a good distance up in the mountains, so it will take a while to get there. You can spend the night at my home with me, if you like. My house is at the foot of the mountains, which is about sixty miles from here. It could change your life and who knows, it might help you to see more clearly where you are heading. So what do you say?" asked Mr. Crossroads.

Mark, pausing to think for a few

moments, took in the atmosphere of the café and the people at the tables. After a short while, he replied, "Well, I had planned to be in Journeytown by tomorrow evening, but I have been waiting all my life for this moment, so I guess another couple of days will not make that much difference." Mark really wanted to see this other road and find out what this cost thing was all about. He was really curious now and it seemed like it might be an exciting adventure. What if he made it to the destiny he wanted, but in the end it was only a facade. So many thoughts and feelings began flooding his mind as he pondered the words of Mr. Crossroads. A few more days would give him some more time to rest from his driving and maybe he could make a better decision, and besides, he really loved the mountains and would love a chance to do some more exploring.

Bill was ecstatic and interrupted the story, "You mean you actually took the time to go out of your way to talk to a stranger you had never seen before and then stay at his house overnight? That must have taken some deep faith. I don't think I could have done that."

Mr. Wisdom replied understandingly, "You see Bill, there was something gentle about this man and the way that he spoke to me. I could sense that he was genuine and that he really cared for me. A few more days on this journey was not really going to matter all that much and besides, I would have more information to make a better choice than what I had learned so far."

"Yeah, maybe so, but weren't you afraid of going alone with a stranger?" asked Bill. Bill didn't trust many people at all. He had such a hard life growing up. His dad had left his mother when he was very young and so he was very insecure in a lot of his relationships. It takes him a while to develop a relationship with certain people, especially strangers. In fact, it had taken him a long time to decide to speak to Mr. Wisdom. He wanted to be sure he was for real, but once he had found out, he was determined to have this meeting.

Mr. Wisdom replied understandingly, "No Bill, you see, as Mr. Crossroads came over and talked with me, I noticed others watching him. I saw the respect they had for him in their eyes. I saw their love for him in the expressions on their faces. I knew I would be safe if I went with him. In fact, I had a feeling of losing out if I didn't go with him. It was really easy to make that decision."

"So, what happened next?" asked Bill, anxious to hear the rest.

"Well," said Mr. Wisdom, "we sat at the café and talked for several hours and then he bought me lunch. After we had eaten, we left for his home. I followed his four-wheel drive pickup in my roadster. It was a beautiful trip up to his place. The roads were winding through the forest, around a lake and over some sheer cliffs. I didn't realize it would take as long as it did, but finally we made it to the entrance to his home. I say home, but it was really a huge, beautiful mansion nestled in among the trees. There was a gushing waterfall over to the left that fell about seventy-five feet into the stream below. The stream was crystal clear and had a deep blue tint to it. It crossed under a huge, stone bridge on his driveway and went into a beautiful pond to the right. There were horses running down by the pond and even a colt that could not have been more than a few weeks old. Beyond the horse barn, in the distance was a medium-sized herd of longhorn cattle. Grazing with the cattle was a small herd of deer. His place wasn't overly done. In fact, it was very modest with the exception of it covering such a huge area of land. All the stone used in the structures and fences had been brought in from the surrounding mountains. They even had a large pool on the side of the house that was heated naturally by the warm springs underground. It seemed like I had found paradise."

"For the first time in my life I felt a peace around me that I had never felt before. I saw a beauty that I had never seen before nor imagined. I wanted to find out more about this man and everything that he had to share with me. I wanted to leave this place a different person. I wanted to take this peace with me. The longer I was there the more I wanted of what I felt around me. My life was already changing and this was only the beginning."

"As I drove further on I noticed a stone entrance that had a bronze plaque at the top of the arch and stopped to read what it said. It read, 'Stand at the crossroads and look; ask for the ancient paths, ask where the good way is, and walk in it, and you will find rest for your soul'."₁

"I was really intrigued by the sign and wondered what the saying meant. It was not going to be too long and I would totally understand its meaning."

"As I drove the rest of the way down his driveway to the house, I reflected back on my life. I grew up in a small town where I knew most of the people. The town had a few factories that kept the local economy going, but that was all. There was also farming and ranching, but most of the people lived just above the poverty line. There were all the usual things available to get young people in trouble. Drugs were available and most of the adults either seemed oblivious to it or were also involved. There was not a lot to do on the weekends so most of the people drove to a neighboring town for entertainment. Life was quite simple in those days. We had phones that had party lines. It was not until I was in my teens that my family actually got a private line. We grew up with black and white TV's and the color TV's didn't come out until I was close to ten."

"Hollywood captured my attention as well as the big cities. There just seemed to be a lot more to do in a big city. I had these big dreams of helping people and creating new inventions. I wanted a better and more challenging life."

"I believed, that in the big city, people didn't know all the intimate details of your life. At least we all had the same chance to make a new start. In the small towns, once you made a mistake it seemed as though you were branded for life. I had made some mistakes and I wanted so desperately to just leave it all behind. I wanted another chance to start over again. I wanted to be free from other's judgments and opinions. They really didn't know me at all. All they saw was the outside, but I knew what I wanted and I was not going to stop until I succeeded. I couldn't give up. This dream just burned within me. It was as if it was driving me on. I had to find out what it was all about. I had to know more and I was not going to find it where I was."

The Crossroad's Home
Illustration by - Krystal Morgan Stahl

Chapter 3

A Life Changing Experience

"I sure wish I could have been there. It sounds incredible! What did his house look like, and his estate?" asked Bill. He was totally engrossed in the story. He would have given anything to have been there with Mr. Wisdom. He wanted to hear more. He made sure, through his body language to let Mr. Wisdom know he was totally interested. He did not want him to skip anything.

"Well," Mr. Wisdom continued. He was so thrilled that Bill was wanting to hear his story. "After I went through the entrance way, I could see that it continued as a stone wall around the perimeter of his house. It must have enclosed ten acres or more of land. There were tall and majestic trees all around, different sized ponds here and there and running water. The birds were singing their songs. They seemed to be singing to me. I began to hear sounds that brought peace to my soul. As the water cascaded down over the cliff, it seemed to be cleansing my soul. The birds seemed to be praising God with their songs as they flitted to and fro from the trees and bushes. The trees themselves seemed to be speaking to me as the wind gently blew through their leaves and branches."

"His house was three stories tall and had thirty-two luxurious bedrooms. The snow-capped mountains rose up from behind the house like a giant painting. It reminded me of a large hotel nestled up in the mountains. I wondered why he would need such a huge place. I parked my car in one of his parking garages. He had quite a collection of different vehicles from around the world. They were all in mint condition. The more I looked around outside the more excited I became about going inside. What was beyond the front door?"

"Most of the ceilings were ten and twelve feet high except for the entrance way, which seemed to arch to the top of the roof. The floors were made of hardwood from many different parts of the world. As I entered into many of the rooms it seemed as though I walked through a portal into another part of the world. Each room was adorned with trinkets, art, pottery, portraits, furniture, linens, and pictures from the country or nation it represented. It was as if you could walk into a different country just by walking into another room. There was even a change in the atmosphere of each room. It was like you could feel the culture of that particular place."

"Wow! That is neat," exclaimed Bill! "What an awesome sidetrack to your stressful journey. You began your journey in one direction and found something better along the way. It sounds like your emotional state was becoming one of ecstasy."

"Yes it was," said Mr. Wisdom, "but that is not even the beginning. As I sat before this giant, granite fireplace with a cup of specially brewed coffee from South America that Mrs. Crossroads had handed me, Mr. Crossroads began to talk to me. The things that he would tell me would forge a new foundation in me that would help carve out a path for me to walk for the rest of my life. I carry these truths with me even to this day and they are as vivid today as they were then. In fact, it is the reason that you see all of this and feel what you feel here. My decision to wait a few days was the best decision of my life. Everything I have successfully built thus far began that day. The decisions I made on that journey became the very foundation that my entire life is built upon. I am so glad I took the time to listen to someone who knew the truth, rather than rush headlong into some of the things that would have certainly brought destruction in my life. I can see now with certainty some of the pitfalls that would have come my way. I am just so grateful that someone took the time and effort to help me along my journey."

"What a difference a single choice can make in someone's life. One moment you can be going down a road to a particular destination and then someone talks you in to taking some time out and all of a sudden your whole life and purpose changes," said Bill. "I guess the real trick is knowing when is the right moment."

"That is right, Bill!" exclaimed Mr. Wisdom. "It is just like you did this morning. Nothing in this world happens to us by coincidence. Sometimes there is a still small voice that speaks inside of our soul. When we hear it, we will do well to obey. Many people are so busy that the noises around them, in their minds and in their thoughts obliterate their view of their path to freedom and they continue to search and search, while never realizing the answer lies within. If they would only stop for a moment, quiet their minds and just listen, they might be able to hear the still small voice inside of their heart. The one that can show them the way."

"Wow!" exclaimed Bill. "I never saw it that way. When I was concentrating on my destiny, it kept me going night and day. It was all I could think about. It was like I was being driven. I just wanted to arrive as soon as possible so I could just rest a bit. It was that passion that was consuming me."

"Passion can be good and very useful if it is ignited by True Love," began Mr. Wisdom. "However, if it is for selfish desires and greed it can cause grief beyond measure. So many people never get the chance to see this side of life. It is so unfortunate, but they won't humble themselves and think that maybe, just maybe, they don't know everything. Maybe there is something better. Maybe there is more to this life than what they have experienced. Maybe there is more than what society itself proclaims and the institutions teach."

"Why is it so hard?" asked Bill seriously.

"It is not really hard at all, rather it is all about choices. You made a choice this morning. You could have just said 'hi' and kept on walking."

"Yes, but I have been waiting for this opportunity to talk to you for a long time.

There were times I would lay awake in bed at night and wonder if I would ever get this opportunity. I wanted to meet you and find out how you got to this place in your life, so I was ready for it," said Bill passionately.

"Sure, I agree. You really wanted something worthwhile for your life. You also checked things out and watched what was going on around you. While you were headed for the things you longed for, you also kept your ears open to the fact that you might not have all the answers. Somewhere in your heart you made the choice to find the truth, even if you were unaware of it. It would not have mattered if you had never met me. You would have searched until you found it. That my friend is the difference between those who find the truth and those who do not. You have to make a conscious decision to search for it no matter what it costs. You must also be willing to wait until it knocks on your door. It is not always going to happen at the most opportune moment, take for instance this morning. It is at that moment you must open the door and take full advantage of the situation. It is only the truth that can make a good change in your life. Now, let's get back to my story about Mr. Crossroads and the next step of the journey."

The Path and the Mountains
Illustration by - Krystal Morgan Stahl

Chapter 4

At The Crossroads, Two Paths

Once we were inside of his home, Mr. Crossroads began his story, "You see, Mark, there are really two paths in this life you can take to reach your destiny. One path is traveled far more than the other one and is the larger of the two. The other path is almost hidden from view and those who go running blindly to find their destiny, just pass right by it. They completely miss it in their rush to grab one illusion after another."

"Yes sir, kind of like I almost did this morning," interrupted Mark. "Had it not been for you, I would not have even known there was another way."

Mr. Crossroads replied, "Thank you, Mark, for your kindness, but there are many who stop at my café in town. I go over and talk to them just like I did with you, but they are in such a hurry that many of them do not even want to talk to me or when they do, they make up some reason why they do not have the time to spend with me. So, they go on their way only to face calamity down the road. They run right into one of the traps or pits that have been placed in the road on the other side of this mountain. I have some friends there who pull them out and try to help them, but sometimes it is just too late. It is a terrible tragedy that could have been avoided had they just stopped for a while and listened. One or two days is not very long when you look at eternity or even just a lifetime on this earth. I do the best I can, but in the end it was their decision and they alone are responsible."

Mark asked, "Can't they see that you only want to help them. I mean, I saw the respect and love that the others in the café had for you. Don't they see it too?"

"I am afraid not, Mark," said Mr. Crossroads. "Many have been blinded by the lies that others have told them about me. Some are so wounded and hurt inside that they do not trust anyone anymore. Some are so prideful that they think they know more than anyone else and they are usually the ones that drive right off of the cliffs and are never seen again. Others are so set in their ways that they can not see anything to the left or right, yet they keep going around in circles, never getting anywhere. All I can do is try to show those who will listen that there is another path they can take. They do not have to listen to the crowd and to those around them. They can make their own choices and it is okay. People do not understand that this path is really not visible until you get up here to the crossroads. Many try to take the shortcut, but they always end up back where they started or worse. Some actually go backwards by getting hurt and wounded. They lose countless years of their lives simply because they

would not slow down and take the time to see if there was another way. It is so sad and frustrating. Sometimes I get depressed when I think about all of those who were lost and I could not do anything else to help them. I know that it is not my fault, but it still does not keep me from feeling that somehow I could have done something more. No one deserves this kind of fate. They deserve better than this and it is this compassion and love that keeps me going. I can not stop. I keep thinking, 'if I can help just one more.'"

In total amazement, Mark said, "What a story. I did not know you felt this way, however, it is evident how much you love others. It is written all over your face So, you mean that I have not even seen this path you have been talking about yet? I thought the path was the road we took to get up here and all this time I thought I was already on my way."

"No, my son," said Mr. Crossroads, "in the morning we will go up to my friend's house, to the top of this mountain and

then you will see the crossroads and the path that I am speaking about, but for tonight you will need to get a good night's rest, because you will need your strength tomorrow for the journey ahead. My staff has prepared your room for you. If you need anything else, just ask Gina and she will get it for you. There are some things I need to do yet tonight before I turn in. Good night, Mark!"

Again, Bill interrupted the story, "Wow! This is totally incredible. And to think I would have missed this had I not taken the time this morning. I am just so amazed at how such a simple choice can make such a huge difference. I noticed a tug on my heart several times over the past few years, but it was only this morning that I took the time to find out what it was all about. Please go on."

Mr. Wisdom continued, "Well, the next morning the sun was shining bright as we stepped outside. The rays were sparkling across the water and the horses were enjoying the briskness of the morning.

The birds had already begun to sing their melodies and all the animals were enjoying the morning air. Everywhere I looked, life was being enjoyed. This was such a wonderful journey that I took some extra time to soak up the beauty and majesty I was experiencing. There was nothing I could compare to this moment in time. It was incredible. There was a sense of majesty and awe in the air. There was not anything man-made for miles around with the exception of the few buildings and structures close to the house."

Mr. Crossroads exclaimed, "Mark, do you see this road that goes up behind my house?"

Mark looked in the direction where Mr. Crossroads had pointed. "You mean that road? That looks more like a goat path than a road. It looks like it goes almost straight up."

Mr. Crossroads laughed, "Ha, ha! Yeah, that is the one. It is not as bad as it looks. Once we get up above this ledge it isn't so bad. We can go up most of the way in my Jeep, but the rest of the way we will have to hike. I am glad you were able to get a good night's rest. We should make it up there before it gets dark. It is getting easier to traverse as the season goes on. Sometimes we just have to wait when we get too much snow. It is going to be good to see my old friend again. I have not seen him for a while now. It seems that every year I make fewer and fewer trips up this old mountain. I hope things change soon. This world seems to be getting worse every day and there does not seem to be an end in sight."

Bill interrupted again, "Mr. Wisdom, can you tell me what the trip was like? Was it as steep as you thought it looked and did it really take you all day to make the climb?"

Mr. Wisdom began again, "Sure Bill. When we started out, I really did not think we would ever make it. The path was so steep, but the four-wheel drive kept us going. We went over rocks, around steep cliffs, places I never thought any vehicle could go. Then, as we rounded a curve, I could see that we were coming to the top of the tree line. There was a ledge over to the right and that is where Mr. Crossroads said we would have to stop and walk. It was an awesome view. As we reached the ledge, I looked back down the way we had come and I could see his estate thousands of feet below and the winding road we had traveled to get up here. He showed me that far below was the town where I had met him. It looked so tiny from up here. It was really quite an adventure, because I had never been up in the mountains before. I wished we would have had the camera technology we have today to capture it all. The only drawback to filming though, would have been that a lot of the experience had to do more with the atmosphere and my emotions and those would have been impossible to capture on film."

"It was already early afternoon by the time we had reached the ledge, so we hurriedly put our backpacks on and continued up the trail. The trail had become very narrow and much steeper. I could not see the summit from here, but Mr. Crossroads said we did not have too much further to go. I was trying to take in all the beauty of the day, the climb and the words he had spoken the night before, but not much of what he had said so far made a lot of sense. This whole journey seemed so complex and yet so simple. It was more than I could grasp at the time. I was feeling things inside of my soul that I had never felt before. There was such a peace about me that even my thoughts seemed to be unusually quiet."

"Finally, after what seemed hours, we reached the snow. We went a little further on and walked out onto a plateau. It was a whole new world up here. It was like civilization had not found this place. It was easy to imagine going back in time to a place where time did not exist. It was very quiet and still, yet full of life and the sounds of nature. Everything seemed in total harmony. At the back of this plateau was a huge log cabin. When we had reached the plateau, Mr. Crossroads began talking again. He had been fairly quiet, except to point out a scene or to show me something along the path."

"Mark, I want to fill you in a little about Mr. Success and tell you a little about his background as we hike the next mile to his house," said Mr. Crossroads. "As you get to know him you will understand why he lives up here in this secluded area. A lot of the questions you have will be answered as he shares his stories with you. Do not judge him by his appearance. He is a brilliant man."

"Mr. Success has seen a lot in his time here on this earth. He has taken both paths in his life. He has many scars and he can share with you many things from his experiences. Make sure you listen closely to him and ask him as many of your questions as you want. When it is time to leave, the day after tomorrow, you must make up your mind as to which way you are going to go. It is from my house that you must walk out your decision, for my place is the crossroads and from there lies your destiny. Mr.

Success is a wise man. You will do well to listen to him closely."

Mr. Wisdom, noticing the sun was almost directly overhead asked, "Bill, why don't we go in to the house and get a refill on the coffee."

As they walked into the house they met up with Mrs. Wisdom. She was on her way to inform them that lunch was ready.

They went into the dining room and sat down at the table by the fireplace and Mr. Wisdom continued his story from there. "Bill, I want you to know that this next part is very important, because as I have been relating to you the events in my life, you have been walking with me. It is very important as I relate to you what Mr. Success told me, that you ask me any questions on your mind, so that when I get through you might be able to make your decision. There is no question that is not important. You must realize that even if you do not make a decision, you are making a decision. Again, it is very important that you understand that by not making a decision, you will in reality, have made one. Life continues on and even if you are standing still, you will in the end, have walked a path. The purpose of Mr. Crossroads is to show us the two paths that are ahead of us, each with its own destiny."

Bill exclaimed, "Wow, Mr. Wisdom, this is heavy. I do want to hear the rest of your story. Thank you for taking the time to share with me. You really have a lot of wisdom, just like your name. Again, I am so glad I stopped this morning. This is great!"

By The Fireplace
Illustration by - Krystal Morgan Stahl

Chapter 5

Mark Wisdom Meets Mr. Success

Bill turned to Mrs. Wisdom, "Thank you, Mrs. Wisdom for that wonderful meal. You are an excellent cook."

Mrs. Wisdom replied with a big smile, "You are quite welcome Bill. I pray that you really hear the words that Mark is preparing to tell you. We enjoy being able to share with others some of the things that we have seen during our life."

Mr. Wisdom returned from the study with a folder in his hand, "Bill, Monique made some Mocha Cappuccino for us in the study and there are a few desserts on the coffee table. I hope you like chocolate."

"I sure do, in fact Mocha Cappuccinos are one of my favorite coffees," Bill interjected with a smile. "Of course, I have to limit them because they are not really that good for me."

"I have a nice fire going, so why don't we go in and sit down," said Mr. Wisdom as he led the way to the study.

Bill walked into the room and his gaze was caught up in the beauty of it. "I like this room. It makes me feel so at home here. Thanks for inviting me in. I feel overwhelmed by your hospitality. I hope that someday I may be able to do this for someone else."

Mr. Wisdom was very eager to get on with the story, "someday you will, but for now we must continue on with the story."

"We continued our hike and in a short while we arrived at the front door of the cabin. As we walked up the steps, a gentleman, who must have been somewhere in his sixties or seventies, opened the door. He had a big smile on his face as he extended his hand toward us and began to speak."

Mr. Success said, "Well, Tom, it sure

is good to see you again. It has been quite a long time, in fact, it seems to be getting longer between your trips up here. This is not a good sign! What is keeping you these days? And who is this young lad with you?"

Mr. Crossroads replied with a grin on his face, "It is good to see you again." Tom went over to Mr. Success and gave him a big hug. "Jim, this is Mark Wisdom. I met him down at the café. He is a fine young man and he is only one of the few who will listen to me anymore. Time seems to be accelerating so fast now and everyone seems to be so caught up in themselves that they just don't take the time anymore for the things that are necessary and truly important."

Mr. Success turned to Mark, "Well, it is good to meet you Mark. Please, both of you come in. I saw you headed this way and put a fresh pot of coffee on the stove. I also have hot water and some teas if you would prefer them. Go on in to the study and I will bring it in to you."

Mr. Crossroads spoke out to Mr. Success as he entered the room with the coffee. "It is sure good being up here again. I like this journey the best of all. I really love the high places. It always makes me think I am on another world when we get up here. Everything else just seems to fade away and I really feel closer to the Lord."

Mr. Success spoke as he handed them their coffee, "Here is your coffee, gentlemen. That, my friend, is one of the biggest reasons we live up here."

Mr. Crossroads, as he reached up for his cup said, "Thank you, it sure is good to have something warm. I was starting to get a chill out there."

Mark remarked also, "Yes, I was getting rather cool myself. Thank you, this coffee sure smells good. It is so beautiful up here. This journey seems to just keep getting better and better. I could not have even dreamed of any of this before today."

Mr. Success just grinned as he replied, "Just wait until tomorrow, you have not seen anything yet."

After they had finished their coffee, gotten a bite to eat, and the conversation of past visits was coming to a head, Mr. Crossroads was ready for a good night's rest. The long journey of the day had worn him out. "Well, I am going to get some shut-eye. I will see you two in the morning."

"Good night, see you in the morning too," said Mr. Success.

After Mr. Crossroads had left the room, Mr. Success turned to Mark. "Well Mark, what brings you to the high places?"

Mark was really wanting to make a good impression so he thought for a while before he spoke, "Well sir," he began, "actually Mr. Success, I want to make the best decision I can for my destiny. I did not even know about another path before Mr. Crossroads told me. I decided that it would not hurt to take a couple of days off from my business and busy schedule to see what this is all about."

Mr. Success spoke seriously as he

looked Mark straight in the eyes, "Well Mark, as you heard earlier, there are not many who get this far anymore. Today, everyone wants the easy way and therefore, they miss out on what is most important. I have walked down both paths in life. I have walked the broad path to what it calls success and at the height of my so-called success is where I saw its destiny. 'There is a way that seems right to a man, but in the end it leads to death.'₁ I almost lost my life and my soul in a place I would have regretted for eternity."

"Are you serious?" asked Mark in unbelief. "I thought that success was everything, to have material wealth, a family, to go wherever you wanted, and to be popular."

Mr. Success chuckled, "that, my son, is only one definition of success. You see, the higher I climbed the ladder of success, the more the emptiness inside of me cried out to be filled. I had this big void, this huge hole in my heart and I tried to fill it with material things, relationships, and power, but it only cried out for more. I had everything I wanted and everything money could buy. I actually had more than I could spend. I gave my family everything they needed except the one thing that really mattered."

"One night I was taken to the emergency room of Metro General Hospital with a massive heart attack. As the doctors frantically worked on my heart, I peered into a realm that would change my life forever. It literally scared me so bad that I think I was shaking in my soul."

"Tomorrow, after we reach the summit, I will continue this story. What you see then will change your life forever."

"Have a good night's rest," said Mr. Success as he was putting everything away for the night.

"Good night, Mr. Success," Mark said as he got up to go to his room.

Bill exclaimed, "You mean to tell me that he left you hanging like that? How could you ever go to sleep with all of that on your mind?"

"Bill," said Mr. Wisdom, "do you feel the peace that is here right now in this house?"

"Yes, I can feel it," said Bill. "It is so wonderful. It seems so thick that I believe I can almost touch it."

"The peace I felt that night was greater than it is here," replied Mr. Wisdom. "I went right to sleep. I think the long journey up the mountain also had something to do with it. The next morning, after I woke up and got ready for the day, I noticed all the accomplishments Mr. Success had in the world. There were plaques and pictures from all over the world hanging on the walls and standing up on shelves. There were also photos with him and other distinguished people and much recognition for many accomplishments. I was so impressed to say the least."

"After we all had breakfast, we went outside to get ready for the day. I was so excited and I could hardly wait to start asking questions. I wanted to know everything. This new journey was so intriguing and amazing."

Mr. Success looked over at Mark, "Are you ready for the climb? We have about 1000 feet higher to go and we will be there. Mr. Crossroads decided earlier to hike up to one of his favorite places, so it will be just the two of us."

Mark was eager to go, "Yes sir, I am ready. I have everything packed. Let's go."

"This path is real steep, so watch your footing," said Mr. Success. "Some of these ridges are very jagged and the snow is quite slick in some places, so be very careful where and how you place your feet."

Bill was all excited as he asked, "How long did it take you, and what did you see?" He could hardly wait to hear about what was coming next.

Mr. Wisdom was glad to see Bill's enthusiasm and continued, "After a few hours we made it to the top. It seemed like I was on the top of the world. It looked as though I could see forever in every direction. As I looked back to the tiny town below, I could see two paths leading away from it. One path lead away from this mountain, but was joined by the other that came from Mr. Crossroads house. The other path went the opposite way from Mr. Crossroad's house, but it did not join another path. In fact, it went through many valleys and over other mountains."

"Mark, do you see the path that leads from town, the one that turns away from this mountain," asked Mr. Success?

"Yes," replied Mark.

"That path is a short cut that bypasses the crossroads. Those who take it get to the broad path much quicker, but they never see this other path. "

"Wow! That is the path I was going to take until I met Mr. Crossroads at the café. I would have totally missed seeing everything," Mark said in a trembling voice realizing the terrible choice he almost made.

"That is right, and that would have

been a grave mistake. Once you get to the crossroads, you can see that the path to the left is a broad path. The way is easy and it is well traveled. Most of it is level and easy to walk. It looks and appears far superior to this narrow path on the right, but its way is very deceptive. There are many traps and pits that are placed along the broad way. Those who walk that way rely on what they can see and feel with their natural minds and emotions. They do not understand that the things they are running towards are only mirages that are placed over the traps and pits that will cause them much pain and suffering. Some go around and around that mountain over there never realizing there is no way to the top. They get caught in a continuous loop that goes nowhere and leads them to destruction."

Mark was puzzled, "but I heard that each path has a destiny. Everyone I see along that path seems to be empty inside. It is like they are trying to fill it with things that mean nothing, empty air. What is their destiny?"

"That, my son, is what I am trying to show you," replied Mr. Success. "Do you see that huge crater over there surrounded by the huge gray and ominous looking cloud?"

"If you mean that large ugly looking thing, yes, I do," said Mark, "and it looks like something must be glowing down inside."

"You are right," replied Mr. Success. "There is a fire that burns day and night there, forever. Eventually, those who walk down the broad path will end up there unless they turn around before it is too late and find this narrow path. Some make it as far as retirement before they enter their eternity in that pit. Others enter sooner when they fall into one of those pits along the way. If you look over there, you can see that along one edge, down inside of each pit, is a slide that angles down into the crater. Once someone slips onto the slide they are never seen again. There, in that crater, they will live eternally in torment and

agony."

"I was at the top of the ladder of success, or at least what I thought was success, when the mirage faded and I saw that I had fallen into one of these pits. That night, during my heart attack, I stared eternal hell straight in the face as I looked over the edge. Everything I had worked for all of my life was left behind. I could not take any of it with me. I was losing everything. The emptiness inside was consuming me as I cried out for help."

"What did you say?" asked Mark rather quickly. The story was really getting to him and he really wanted to get past this place.

"Well," said Mr. Success, "back at the beginning of my walk, I had the chance to come up here, but I didn't. I did, however, come to the crossroads and saw that there were two paths. The narrow path looked too boring and too difficult to walk, so I chose the broad way, but in this moment I remembered Mr. Crossroad's father calling out to me,

telling me to call out to the Lord Jesus Christ, that He would help me and show me the way no matter where I was."

"In the depths of that horrible pit, I remembered what he had said and I cried out, 'Lord Jesus, if You are really there and if you are really real, come and save me and show me Your way. I do not want anything more to do with this path. Please help me make it to the other path. Please come and help me. I want to know the truth. I have seen the reality of this path. I am so sorry for not listening to Mr. Crossroads and for choosing to do things my way. Will you please forgive me and have mercy on my. I know I do not deserve it, but please, could you help?'"

"All of a sudden a bright light flashed before me and Jesus appeared. He reached out His hand and a peace filled my body that I had never felt before. I heard the doctors proclaim that all of a sudden my heart was back to normal. They could not believe it. It was as if I had never even had a heart attack. They even *ran all kinds of tests on me. The most amazing thing that happened, that was even better than having my heart healed, was the emptiness that I had felt all of my life was now filled with love. The emptiness was totally gone and also its insatiable, ungratifying appetite. I had met the One Who is love, and He made my life complete. I was different from that point on. I could not explain it, but I knew that I had crossed over that night from eternal death to eternal life. The next morning, when I awoke, I found that I was no longer on the broad path, but now I was on the narrow path. It really felt wonderful. I knew that I had found the truth at last and no one would be able to deceive me again."*

"Because of what He did for me, I would gladly give Him my life and do anything He would ask of me. I decided that day to give Him my life and serve Him the rest of my time here on this earth. I chose to go wherever He said and speak to whomever He said. I am so grateful that He reached down and

gave me a new, wonderful and glorious life. There is nothing I could ever do for Him to ever repay Him, therefore, I choose to love Him with all of my heart and everything that is within me. He has shown me a better way and I will be forever grateful."

The Journey Begins

The Wind Blows
Illustration by - Krystal Morgan Stahl

Chapter 6

Mark Sees A New Way

Mark exclaimed, "Wow! That is incredible! Tell me about this narrow path. Why does it go the way it does? Why does it seem so hard?"

"The narrow path is impossible to walk without the help of the Lord," began Mr. Success. "In fact, unless you are born again, you will not even understand it or even be able to journey on it. It doesn't make sense to the natural mind."

Mark questioned, "What do you mean, born again? How can I be born again?"

"I believe that man is three separate entities in one," replied Mr. Success. "He has a body, which is the flesh and at the end of his life here on earth it will return to dust. He has a soul, which is his *mind, will and emotions. And he has a spirit which is dead because of the sinful nature of man.₁ The spirit of man died at the fall of man in the garden of Eden when he gave in to the temptation of Satan. A man's spirit must be born again in order for him to see the things of the Spirit.₂ God is Spirit. Therefore, in order for us to see the things of the Spirit, our spirits must be alive inside of us. That is the emptiness we feel so strong inside and nothing else can fill it.₃ We can try like I did to fill it, but it only gets worse until we accept the truth. It is a matter of humbling oneself and coming to the knowledge and understanding that we might not know and understand what we think we know. Maybe there is someone who is greater than us. We have to let go of our pride and this is a huge stumbling block to a lot of people."*

"I don't understand," exclaimed Mark.

"Well, it is kind of like this," began Mr. Success. "You hear the wind blowing, but you cannot tell where it is going or

where it is coming from. So it is with those who are born of the Spirit of God. The ways of the Spirit can not be seen with the natural eye, nor can it be understood with the natural mind. You can not see the wind, yet you know it is there. You can not see the Spirit, yet sometimes you know there is something more because you can feel it deep inside."

"So how will I be able to understand these things," asked Mark?

Mr. Success answered, "You must invite Jesus into your heart, to be the Lord and Savior of your life. You must choose to turn away from the sin in your life and choose to follow Jesus wherever He leads you."[4]

"Well," Mark said hesitantly, "I don't know about that. I do not even know this Jesus. Who is He?"

Mr. Success started to explain, "Jesus is the Son of God. He left heaven and came down to earth to show us the way to eternal life. He gave up His glory in heaven and became a man and walked among men.[5] *He was crucified on a*

73

cross though He had never sinned. He was the perfect sacrifice for all of our sins and every sin that we would ever commit. A perfect lamb was needed in the Old Testament of the Bible for the forgiveness of sin. Jesus was the perfect sacrifice, Who once and for all paid the penalty in full for our sins, through His death on the cross and the shedding of His blood.₆ Death could not hold Him in the grave, because He had never sinned. For the wages of sin is death, but the gift of God is eternal life.₇ Therefore He took upon Himself the sin of the world that He might pardon those who accept Him and believe on His Name, and give them eternal life."

"This is wonderful!" exclaimed Mark. "But what if I decide later that I don't want to go that way?"

Mr. Success answered, "You can always turn around and go back. The choice is yours to make, but once you have made the decision to walk this path, you won't want to turn back. Everything will be new to you, and you will see *things in a whole new perspective. This new life is full of joy, love and peace. It is not an easy path, but it is more than worth it."*

"Look on the other side of this mountain and you can see the narrow path below. There are mountains and valleys to cross and when you choose this path you will never be alone. There are trials you will face, but the beauty you find will far exceed the cost.[8,9] Again, I tell you, you will never be alone.[10] Even when you feel like you are, the Lord and His angels will be with you always.[11] As you look toward the end of the path, you can see a golden looking cloud in the distance."

"Yes!" Mark said with delight, "I can see it. What is it?"

Mr. Success continued, "That is the eternal heaven where the throne of God is and His glory. Those who choose the narrow path will find eternal life. They believe and trust in His Son, Jesus Christ.[12] They develop a relationship with Him and walk with Him as their friend. They share their secrets with Him and He with them. He becomes more real to them than their closest friends. They choose to overcome the things of this world and they will inherit the things of God. They will be His people, and God Himself will be with them and be their God and Father. He will wipe every tear from their eyes. There will be no more death or mourning or crying or pain." [13]

"Mark, as you can see, I am truly successful. All of my needs and wants are met and I have love in my heart. I am now complete. I have a peace inside of me that surpasses all understanding. I thought I had lost it all, but I was given another chance. He gives each of us second chances. He does not want anyone to perish. He loves His creation. Love gives the ability to choose. He wants us to love Him because we choose to, not because we have to love Him. This is the definition of love. Without having choices, love can not exist nor would it have any meaning. Love is all about taking chances and when you find

it, you will do all that is in your power to keep it."

"Mr. Success," asked Mark, "how can I receive Jesus into my heart? I want to walk this narrow path of life."

Mr. Success replied understandingly, "Two days from now, when you get back to the crossroads, your journey will continue. Mr. Crossroads will show you where to go and what to do next. You will meet a man whose name is Mr. Witness. When you talk to him, you can tell him of your decision and he will help you continue your journey."

"Let's go back down to my house and get a good night's rest. In the morning you can go back with Mr. Crossroads."

Time to Reflect
Illustration by - Krystal Morgan Stahl

Chapter 7

Mark Meets Mr. Witness

"I didn't know about all of this," said Bill. "This is incredible and to think I could have missed all of this and gone the wrong way because of my busyness. That is funny. What an interesting play on the word business. I wonder if that is how they came up with it in the first place? What did you do next, Mr. Wisdom?"

"Well Bill," said Mr. Wisdom, "I got up the next morning and Mr. Crossroads and I made our trip back to his house. The things, which I had learned in those last two days, overwhelmed me to say the least. We talked about a few things on the journey back, but mostly I wanted to take in the beauty of the scenery. I didn't know if I would be going back up there again, so

I wanted to memorize as much as I could to take with me on my journey."

"That night I had a real peaceful sleep. It was almost as if I were sleeping on a cloud. The next morning I awakened early and ate breakfast. Mr. Crossroads told me about Mr. Witness and how to locate him. He said that I would know who he was when I met him. I thanked Mr. and Mrs. Crossroads for their hospitality and then I was on my way."

"I drove the short distance from his house to the crossroads. I turned in the direction of the narrow path and headed on. After a short distance, I saw a café on the right and felt an inner urge to stop. I stopped my roadster and went in for a cup of coffee. It was almost as if the scene of the other café was happening all over again. A man came over and introduced himself to me as Mr. Witness. After we sat and talked for a while, he asked me to come outside with him."

"Mark," said Mr. Witness, "I would like to show you something outside

if you will follow me." After they had walked out to the side of the building, Mr. Witness looked in the direction of where the road was leading. "If you look up toward where this path is leading, you will see that the grade gets higher. There will be some obstacles in your way. Sometimes you will feel all alone, but know that when you do the Lord is always with you. Holy Spirit will be your inward witness as you navigate along this path. Read His Word, the Bible, and pray always. Your relationship with Him will develop as you stay on this path. Through the obstacles, trials and temptations that come your way, you will learn how to overcome. As you walk, Jesus will become more and more real to you. Eventually, He will be as real to you as any of your friends and even as I am to you."

"I will go with you part of the way to help you get started. Others will come along as you walk and they will also offer their help. There will be times you will help others and there will be times

you will be by yourself."

"There will also be those who will come along and try to lead you astray. Be careful to always pray, read the Word, and to listen to the voice of Holy Spirit. He will lead you to where you need to go. As you become accustomed to hearing Him, His voice will become more and more distinct. You will be able to tell the difference between his voice and the voice of strangers that will whisper in your ears. You will not always do what others are doing, nor will you always go where they are going. You are an individual and Jesus wants to have a personal relationship with you."

"You will walk among many brothers and sisters in the Lord. You will have a new family. With some, you will walk closely like a brother and others will be like friends. There will be a few who will take you under their wing to teach and train you in the ways of the Lord. Imitate their lives in the ways that they glorify the Lord.₁ We all have the same destiny and we must help each other get

there. We are of one family, the children of God."

"I want to invite Jesus into my life right now," exclaimed Mark. "I want to walk down this path He has for me. I want eternal Life."

"All right," said Mr. Witness, "I want you to ask the Lord and I will agree with you and be your witness. Repeat after me, 'Jesus, I want you to come into my life. I ask You to forgive me of my past with sin. I turn away from sin and the works of the devil and I ask You to be the Lord and King of my life. Fill me with Your Spirit that He may guide me and lead me to eternal life. By Your grace, I will walk this path You have before me. I know that You have Your best in mind for me, even when I do not understand. I choose to trust You, help me Lord. I lay down my will for my life and ask that You fulfill the desires You placed in me, even from my birth.$_2$ Thank You, in Jesus' Name, Amen.'"

"Wow!" exclaimed Mark, "I actually feel different. Something really happened.

My heart is not empty anymore. Thank You, Jesus!"

"Mark," said Mr. Witness, "If you would like, you can spend the night at my house and we can start off tomorrow. I will show you a few things tonight that will help you to begin your journey tomorrow."

"Mr. Wisdom," Bill began, "I want to go down this narrow path of life also. What must I do to be saved?"

"Just repeat the prayer like I did to the Lord Jesus Christ. He is right here with us," said Mark Wisdom. The room was suddenly filled with the presence of the Lord. The whole atmosphere had changed.

"Okay!" exclaimed Bill as he finished the prayer in his own words, "I really am different now! I felt the change. The emptiness left. This is incredible. Can you tell me more about this Jesus? Can you help me?"

"Well Bill," said Mr. Wisdom, "it is late tonight, but I tell you what. If you would like, you can take this Bible with you tonight. You can start by reading the gospel of John. If you like, you can stop by in the morning and I will tell you some more and I will help you get started down this narrow path of life where you will find true success. As you read, ask the Lord to make His Word come alive to you."

"You have a deal!" exclaimed Bill, "I will see you tomorrow, Mr. Wisdom. Thank you for taking the time for me. Good night."

"Good night, Bill," said Mr. Wisdom as Bill started walking down the sidewalk to his home.

A Ripple in the Pond
Illustration by - Krystal Morgan Stahl

Chapter 8

A Good Night's Rest

Mark slept well that night, perhaps better than ever before, well, at least after he got to sleep. It was as if the love of the Lord was continually pouring over him like a refreshing mountain stream. All the thoughts and plans of his destiny were changing course. It was not about him and his desires anymore, but what does the Lord want to do with his life. Why was he created? What divine purpose was created just for him? What book would be written as he walked through the pages of his life? Who would see it and how would the fact that he lived change other's courses in history? Could he alone make a positive difference? How many lives would change all because he chose to follow his heart? It was like a pebble being thrown into the water, the ripples affect all the water around it, so would be his life, his destiny. He could hardly wait for morning.

Bill was going through a similar thing as he lay awake in bed. All the things Mr. Wisdom had told him during the day had seemed to be so super real. Could all of this be real? He knew that what he felt when he gave his life to the Lord, was real. There was a real change. Now, he knew the emptiness in his heart had been filled with Love - True Love. This was not like all the ideas and relationships before that promised to be fulfilling only to end in agonizing pain. The hole in his heart had been growing from all the pain in his past, but now it was beginning to heal. Oh! What a wonderful feeling to be free at last. What a wonderful feeling to be truly loved, at peace and not alone anymore.

Then, all of a sudden this wonderful feeling of joy was interrupted by a thought that seemed to come out of nowhere. Julie!

What time was it now? The clock showed 12:39 a.m. She was in Chicago finishing up her last year in college and in all that was going on today, he completely forgot about calling her tonight. She was trying to get things finished there so she could move in permanently with him. They were planning to get married in the summer.

He jumped out of bed to see if she had left him a message, but there were not any messages for him. This day had been particularly quiet. Well, at least he didn't miss her call. He decided he would call her first thing in the morning before she left for her first class.

She was a very special lady to him. He had other relationships before this, but they all ended up bad. He had been reluctant to date again, but as he and Julie became friends, it became apparent to both of them that their relationship was much deeper than friendship. They had been dating for the last year and a half. Bill had graduated last year and found a job here in Colorado, so he moved out here and now they see each other every other weekend. During the Christmas break they decided that Julie would move into his apartment as soon as she finished in May. Their wedding was only five months away, so it shouldn't be any big deal. Bill had some reservations at first, but after much coaxing by Julie he agreed. It was not like they were not going to get married and each of them had different relationships before.

But now, his thoughts were interrupted again. He had always heard, while he was growing up, that sex before marriage was wrong. All of a sudden the guilt enveloped him and then confusion.

"Lord, do you still love me? What do I need to do now?"

What will Julie think? What a mess. If I change my mind now, will she leave me. She might even get really hurt? I don't want to hurt her. She has been through enough as it is. As for that matter, so have I. "Lord, I don't know what to do? Please help me to make the right decision."

Anxiety had gripped his heart and for the first time in a long time he felt that ominous feeling of fear again. He could feel it crawling up his back and all the way up to his neck. All he could see was Julie crying and walking away. Was it over? Would she be able to see the change in him and want what he has or would she totally reject him? His peace and freedom had left him and now the fear became a prison that locked him in a room inside of his heart. He had been there before, but that had been a while back. Now, things seemed all too familiar again. Destiny, the dream, the journey, he had to refocus because he knew where this path of fear led and he didn't want anything to do with it. He turned over on his pillow and the tears began to flow.

After a while had passed, he looked up and there stood the Lord at the side of his bed. "Bill," He said, "let Me comfort you. Just receive my love and rest for tonight."

Once again the peace returned and he drifted off to sleep.

A Choice Must Be Made
Illustration by - Krystal Morgan Stahl

Chapter 9

A Brand New Day

Bill awoke at 5:57 the next morning before his alarm went off. He had two things on his mind. First, he wanted to spend some time reading in the Bible and second, he wanted to call Julie before 8:00 o'clock.

He started reading in the book of John and began to learn more about this Jesus and His love for His people. He thought, 'was last night a dream or was Jesus really standing by my bed? No, it was real because I felt the peace and I still feel it now.'

"Thank you Lord, You are special."

The next thought that came into his mind was, "Bill, You are special to Me too. I saw your face that night in Gethsemane along with others and again while I was on the cross and I knew then My death would not be in vain. I saw this day too and it brought me much joy."

The next time Bill looked up from his reading it was 7:45. He quickly went to the phone and called Julie but there wasn't any answer. He left her a message letting her know that he loved her and that he would call later. In a way, he was relieved, because he didn't know quite what to say. Everything was different now and he really did not want to talk to her long distance. He wanted to be there in person. Maybe he just needed to fly there and see her. He thought for a moment longer as he meditated on all the changes that one day had made in his life and then decided it was time to go and see Mr. Wisdom again.

As Bill walked up to the gate, Mr. Wisdom looked up from the newspaper he was reading while he was swinging on the porch swing. "Good morning Bill," said Mr. Wisdom enthusiastically.

"Good morning, Mr. Wisdom," replied

Bill. "It really is a gorgeous day today, and this time I took in everything as I walked over. The birds are so cheerful that one can't help but have their spirit lifted just by listening to their wonderful melodies."

"I agree Bill, but there are many who don't listen with their hearts and so the encouragement from our heavenly Father goes unnoticed to them. He reaches out to touch their hearts, but they are oblivious," spoke Mr. Wisdom.

"How do you know that?" asked Bill. "How do you know so much?"

"I was one of them once," said Mr. Wisdom. "Well, come on around back and let's enjoy the presence of the Lord again, shall we?"

"I am all excited, but there are some serious things I have to ask you this morning. I need some answers before I talk to Julie this evening," said Bill. "I am in a desperate situation and I just don't know what to do. Can you help?"

"Well son," began Mr. Wisdom, "I probably can, but why don't we see what Father has to say. I would rather hear His word on the matter. He knows what is best." They walked up the steps at the back of the house to the veranda. Then they sat down at an old iron table that had a pretty green-laced tablecloth on top. "Bill, are you thirsty? I just made some Green tea. Would you like a cup? There is also some Breakfast Blend or some French coffee."

"I would love to try the Green tea. I have heard a lot about it. Do you have any honey?" asked Bill.

"Sure, it is over by the coffee, help yourself," replied Mr. Wisdom. "How about a multi grain raisin muffin to go along with that tea?"

"Sounds great! Boy, talk about a healthy start to the morning! Thank you," said Bill.

"Your welcome," replied Mr. Wisdom. After they sat down and talked again about the wonderful scenery of the mountains, the lake, and the ducks, Mr. Wisdom asked, "Now what was it that you wanted to ask me?"

"Mr. Wisdom, before I went to sleep last night I began thinking of my relationship with Julie. I know that you are aware of our living arrangements and last night this incredible amount of fear just gripped my heart when I was faced with trying to make a right decision concerning her. Above all, I do not want to hurt or lose her." Bill told Mr. Wisdom the details of the night before and how Jesus appeared and he was able to get to sleep. He also told him what had happened this morning.

"Wow!" said Mr. Wisdom, "What a story. Sounds to me that the Lord is serious about you knowing that He loves you. The battle for your mind is getting really serious. Father has exposed a place in your heart where the enemy has had you bound for years."

"What do you mean?" asked Bill. "How am I bound? I don't have any ropes around me, at least none that I can see."

"There is fear in your heart, just as there is some fear in everyone's heart; fear of failure, fear of success, fear of happiness, fear of relationships, fear of loss, and on and on. Most people wear a mask of some kind or another, hoping no one will see some of their innermost secrets, however, rest assured, there are two for sure who know what is there," said Mr. Wisdom.

"The Lord for one," interrupted Bill. "He was with me last night, but who is the other one?"

"The devil of course!" said Mr. Wisdom. Scripture talks a lot about our enemy and how he hates mankind and is constantly trying to destroy us. Most of Jesus' ministry, while He was on the earth, was dealing with him and casting him out so people could be free and healed."

"Wow! Kind of like Star Wars, huh?" asked Bill.

"What do you mean?" asked Mr. Wisdom.

"Well, you know, the good versus evil thing," replied Bill.

"Only in a small sense of the word, because Star Wars only focuses on a humanistic view of good versus evil. It has no real answers, however it has a good story line and focuses on good always triumphing over evil. There are a lot of good things we can gain from the movies, but you must also realize that with God, Jesus is the focal point. He is the hero and if we want to do anything worthwhile on this earth, it will only happen when we surrender to Him and walk in His strength and power," said Mr. Wisdom seriously.

"I thought that God helps those who help themselves," said Bill.

"Show me where it is in His Word that He says that," said Mr. Wisdom.

"I don't know, but I have heard a lot of people say that," said Bill.

"Unfortunately, you can not believe everything you hear, even if it comes from another Christian. God helps the helpless and those who know that without Him they can accomplish nothing," said Mr. Wisdom. "God helps the humble, but He opposes the proud. Paul states it this way, 'it is when I am weak then I am strong.'"

"Sounds like a contradiction to me," replied Bill.

"I know it does Bill, but believe me, I have been there. In my youth, there didn't seem to be anything I could not do and because of that belief, my pride became way too big. It actually got in my way. Father, in His loving kindness, allowed me to go through a period when nothing I did prospered. I had the skills and I had done certain things before, but there was a time when nothing worked, no matter how hard I tried. It was then I realized who I was and Who He really is," said Mr. Wisdom.

"Well, what about my situation with Julie. How is it going to work out? I do not know what to do. I don't want to lose her or even more than that, see her hurt," Bill said very seriously.

"I really don't know how it is going to work out," said Mr. Wisdom. "How do you want it to work out?"

"I want everything to be great and wonderful. I want her to see the Lord as I do and for her to give her life to Him too," said Bill.

"It might work out that way, but what if it doesn't Bill?" asked Mr. Wisdom. "Are you prepared for what might happen?"

"But God would not do that to me, would He?" asked Bill.

"Father doesn't have anything to do with that part. He has given everyone a free choice. He didn't create a bunch of robots to do His every command. He wants His creation to love Him and do things based on this love for Him," said Mr. Wisdom. "Julie has a free choice, however, we can pray that Father will show her the truth and protect her from the deceitfulness and lies of the enemy."

"I don't know what I will do if I lose her!" exclaimed Bill sorrowfully.

"Now Bill, we have not even crossed that bridge yet. Let's not make this situation harder than it has to be, okay? The biggest question of all is who do you value more? Who means more to you?" asked Mr. Wisdom.

"You mean I have to make a choice?" asked Bill.

"Life is always about making choices. First of all, Who created you?" asked Mr. Wisdom.

"Jesus, of course," said Bill.

"Who knows your purpose on this earth?" asked Mr. Wisdom.

"Jesus," replied Bill.

"Then, don't you think He also cares about your heart? What about last night, when you were in the middle of all that fear and heartache, Who was it that comforted your heart?" asked Mr. Wisdom.

"He came and filled me with His peace," said Bill.

"He is trying to show you that He cares for you and that no matter what happens with this relationship it will work out for the best," said Mr. Wisdom.

"But, what if she walks away?" asked Bill. "I don't think I could make it through that again."

"What are you going to do if she makes you choose, Bill?" asked Mr. Wisdom.

"I have to follow Jesus. He is the One Who saved me and gave His life for me. I can't turn away from Him. I have to trust that He knows what is best for my life," said Bill. "I am going to fly up in the morning and see her in person. She needs to see the change in me. I can't do this over the phone."

"What about the change in your

relationship in regards to intimacy?" asked Mr. Wisdom.

"I don't know yet. Hopefully, she can see that I am not rejecting her, but rather it is all about love and respect. I have not treated her righteously. She deserves more and I owe her that. I love her so much," said Bill.

Mr. Wisdom began, "Bill, let me tell you about what happened to me as I was just beginning my new journey with the Lord . . ."

Joseph James

AUTHOR'S COMMENTS

What about you, the reader of this book? Did you find yourself agreeing with the emptiness you feel inside; the wanting to be loved for who you are and not having to perform for that love or having the need to control love? Dear friend, only Jesus can fill that emptiness inside of you. No human being can love you the way you need to be loved. And truthfully, we don't even know what love is until we invite Him, Who is Love into our hearts.

Jesus Christ is real. You might not be able to see Him, but He is reality. The journey, in this book, was taken by fictitious characters, however I did use excerpts from the lives of those I have known personally and some from my own life experiences.

The only way to eternal life is through Jesus Christ. He said, "I am the Way, the Truth, and the Life" (John 14:6) NIV. The part in parenthesis means that this verse is found in the book of John in the Bible, chapter 14 and verse 6. The NIV stands for the New International Version of the Bible. John also wrote, "Yet to all who received Him, to those who believed in His Name, He gave the right to become children of God" (John 1:12) NIV. In (John 10:10) NIV, Jesus said, "the thief, (Satan, the devil), comes only to steal and kill and destroy; I have come that they may have life, and have it to the full."

The devil tries to lie to us through any means he can. Only the truth, the Word of God, can dispel the devil's lies. The devil tries to pull us away through false doctrines (beliefs), the methods of man, and the doctrines of demons and cults.

Dear friend, if you want to know Jesus personally, pray the prayer that Mark Wisdom and Bill Solomon prayed. Just ask Him. Once you do and He comes into your heart, get a Bible and start reading the New Testament first. Read the book of John. I suggest that you read the New Testament several times, the Psalms, and the Proverbs before starting the Old Testament. Ask Holy Spirit to reveal to you the words you are reading and He will. The Bible will become more to you than just a textbook. It will become a book of life to you.

In (1John 2:27), another book that John wrote, located close to the book of Revelation, John states, "the anointing, (the Holy Spirit), you received from Him remains in you, and you do not need anyone to teach you. But as His anointing teaches you about all things and as that anointing is real, not counterfeit – just as it has taught you, remain in Him." John was writing to warn us against those who appear to be teachers of the gospel, but their main purpose is to lead others astray. The Lord will show you which Christian fellowship to go to and who to listen to, if you ask Him. Unfortunately, not every one who calls himself a Christian is one. Keep your focus on Jesus and keep reading His Word. If you have a genuine desire to find the truth, and you look for it with all your heart, you will find it.

When you look for a Bible, I suggest you try to find one of the following versions: the New American Standard, (NAS); the New International Version, (NIV); the New King

James, (NKJ) or the Amplified Bible. The King James, (KJ), is written in Old English style and is much harder to understand when first beginning. Also, a concordance of the Bible is very helpful. This will give you a more in-depth understanding of the words and their meanings.

If you desire, you can contact us at: www.destinypathoflife.com. Just use the form on the contact page. We would like to hear from you. The address is at the front of this book if you want to write by snail mail. May the Lord draw you ever deeper into His love. May His peace fill your life. Jesus cares and so do we.

Joseph James

A P P E N D I X

COVER & CHAPTER 2

1. (Jeremiah 6:16) NIV

CHAPTER 5

1. (Proverbs 16:25) NIV

CHAPTER 6

1. Ref. (Genesis 3)
2. Ref. (John 3:1-8)
3. Ref. (Ephesians 2:1-10)
4. Ref. (Romans 10:9,10)
5. Ref. (Philippians 2:5-11)
6. Ref. (Hebrews 9)
7. (Romans 6:23) NIV
8. Ref. (Isaiah 43:1,2)
9. Ref. (Hebrews 12:2)
10. Ref. (Hebrews 13:5)
11. Ref. (Psalms 91)
12. Ref. (Matthew 7:13,14)
13. Ref. (Revelation 21:1-7) NIV

CHAPTER 7

1. Ref. (Hebrews 6:12)
2. Ref. (Jeremiah 1:5)

About The Author

Joseph grew up in a small town in South Central Texas, USA in the sixties. He says he was fortunate to grow up in the country, because it helped him overcome the absence of his father. His father left his mom when he was three. Sometimes, he would walk for hours at a time as a child throughout the countryside in order to find peace and tranquility. He observed the animals in the wild and took note of how they lived and interacted. He also learned first hand about plants, farming, and ranching. It was during these times that He came to realize the Lord was real. Later in life, he would meditate on these precious times to help encourage himself, especially when living in the large cities of San Antonio and Dallas.

He is a passionate writer, songwriter, singer, and artist. He loves to create things and write stories that can help encourage others. He also writes in his blog on www. destinypathoflife.com when he can.

He understands what it is like to live

in torn family relationships. He has had to lean totally on the Lord to help him make it through each day. He speaks directly from His relationship with the Lord.

Please feel free to visit our web sites at: www.DestinyPathOfLife.com, www.BeneficialZone.com and www.VaryMedia.com. If you would like to contact us, please send any correspondence to the address at the front of the book or use the contact form on either of these three sites.

Thank you for reading this book. We hope it has helped you in some way. Our goal is to help others, to encourage them and help them to find their destiny. There are several tools available on the Destiny web site. There is a questionnaire available to help determine one's talents and gifts. There is also an art print, books, music, and a flash jukebox with two of Joseph's songs. As time and funding become available we will be producing more of his songs for your listening. He is currently working on two more books and will be working on the sequels to this one in the near future.

May your life be blessed by the Lord.

May you continue to walk deeper and deeper with Him. May He become your best friend. Rise above the things that would try to keep you down and soar high above on His wings of love.

Special For You!

Be sure to visit our ***DestinyPathOfLife.com*** web site to download a desktop wallpaper of your choice for free. These will be available in print, sometime in the near future.

 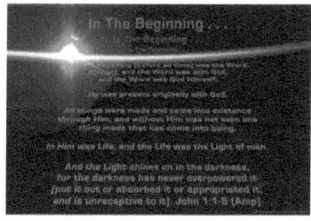

Also, be sure to visit our ***BeneficialZone. com***. This is our e-commerce site where purchases of this book can be made as well as other beneficial products. Subscribe to our blogs on both sites to keep up with the latest news and visit often for the newest additions and changes.

Visit ***VaryMedia.com*** for any graphic & web design as well as any publishing information.

Destiny Path Of Life™ Art Print

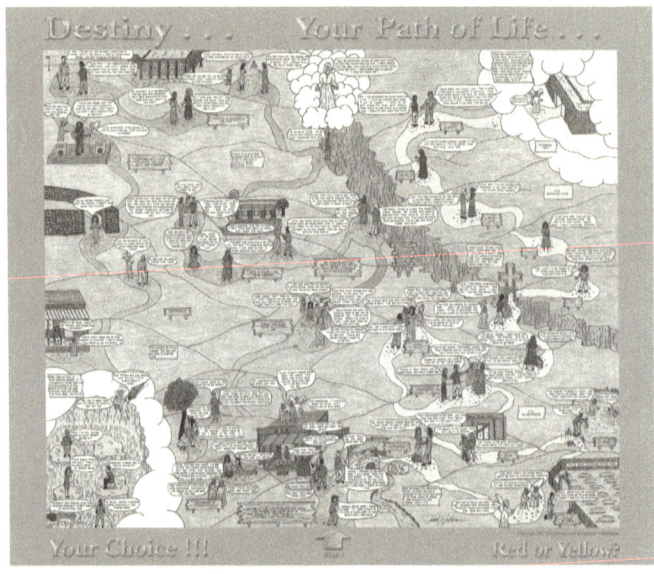

Joseph has created an art print that goes along with this book and also its sequels. Discover the two paths in life. Journey down each path and discover some of the truths and pitfalls in life. Face the crossroads and decide for yourself. Visit our web site for more details and availability.

Take the journey,
Share the ride,
Climb the mountain,
Then decide!